The Sleepover Club

Have you been invited to all these sleepovers?

The Sleepover Club
Goes for Goal!

by Fiona Cummings

An imprint of HarperCollinsPublishers

The Sleepover Club ® is a
registered trademark of HarperCollins*Publishers* Ltd

First published in Great Britain by Collins in 1999
Collins is an imprint of HarperCollins*Publishers* Ltd
77-85 Fulham Palace Road, Hammersmith,
London, W6 8JB

The HarperCollins website address is
www.**fireandwater**.com

3 5 7 9 8 6 4

Text copyright © Fiona Cummings 1999

Original series characters, plotlines
and settings © Rose Impey 1997

ISBN 0 00675447-3

The author asserts the moral right to
be identified as the author of the work.

Printed and bound in Great Britain by
Omnia Books Limited,
Glasgow

Sleepover Kit List

1. Sleeping bag
2. Pillow
3. Pyjamas or a nightdress
4. Slippers
5. Toothbrush, toothpaste, soap etc
6. Towel
7. Teddy
8. A creepy story
9. Food for a midnight feast:
   chocolate, crisps, sweets, biscuits.
   In fact anything you like to eat.
10. Torch
11. Hairbrush
12. Hair things like a bobble or hairband,
    if you need them
13. Clean knickers and socks
14. Change of clothes for the next day
15. Sleepover diary and membership card

CHAPTER ONE

She turns, she shoots, she scores! *Yeeaah!* Kenny for England, Kenny for England! Whoops, sorry, I didn't see you there. Blinding shot, wasn't it? But what do you expect? I am a footballing genius after all!

Actually, I'm just getting in a bit of practice before the others get here for a kick-around. Why are you looking at me like that? Yes I do mean the rest of the Sleepover Club, what's so strange about that? But of course, you don't know do you? *Cool!* I'm going to love telling you about our latest Sleepover adventure. You're never going to believe it. Never in a million years!

As you know, I think that football is the best game in the world, and I can't understand people who don't. But it seems that the others thought *I* was the one who was weird. Now I suppose I can understand Fliss for having that attitude because, well – she's so *girly*, basically. I mean, mud and Fliss just don't go. She complains when it's cold. She complains when it's wet. And there's no way that you'd get her running about outside in a skimpy pair of shorts messing up her hair. The only good thing about football as far as Fliss is concerned is David Beckham. And the only reason she knows about him is because she's seen posters of him in stupid girly magazines. As I say, I sort of see where she's coming from, but the others? I just don't understand them at all.

Take Frankie. She's my best mate and you'd think that she'd agree with me about the most important thing in my life, wouldn't you? Well, you couldn't be more wrong. She says she can't see the point of football at all. But that's just crazy, because she plays netball and she thinks that's OK. And football's the same, isn't it? Apart from the fact that you kick the ball – and you have goals instead of nets – and the pitch is bigger… Look, what I mean is, in both games whoever scores the most wins, right? So basically they're the same. Everybody thinks that Frankie is some brainbox or something, but if you ask me, sometimes she can be really dumb!

Rosie's the same. Her brother Adam is crazy about football, but all she does is wind me up by calling me a hooligan. Just because I go to watch Leicester City with my dad. As far as she's concerned, it's as though every single football supporter goes around beating up old grannies in their spare time. My dad's a doctor for goodness sake, and he's not violent at all. He never even shouts out anything rude at a match. And sometimes Leicester City play so badly they deserve to be shouted at, believe me!

The person I *really* can't understand though is Lyndz. She goes to football matches with her grandad and her brothers sometimes. We all sit together. She *loves* going. I know she does, because she gets all excited and jiggles about in her seat. You ought to hear her when someone scores a goal. But in front of the others she always pretends that she's not that interested. You just can't work some people out, can you?

But really, the fact that I love football so much has never been that big a deal. It's just a fact of life that the others accept. Or at least, that *was* the case. All that changed when the notice appeared at school.

Now you should know that as soon as a new notice goes up everybody crowds round, as though it's some really important event. I know, I know, it's a bit sad isn't it? Well anyway, one Monday, there was this big crush in the corridor at the end of lunchtime break.

"Looks like there's a new notice up!" said Frankie, elbowing her way to the front of the crowd.

"Hope it's something exciting!" Rosie shouted, joining her.

Fliss, Lyndz and I didn't want to feel left out, so we got some serious elbow action going and worked our way to the front to join the others.

There was a bright spanking new notice up, but somehow the others weren't impressed. As soon as Fliss read it she turned away in disgust.

"If I'd known it was going to be so boring, I wouldn't have wasted all that energy!" she sniffed, and pushed her way back out through the crowd again. The others followed her. But it was one of the best notices I'd ever read, so I stayed there a bit longer just staring at it. It said:

FIVE-A-SIDE PRACTICES

Wednesdays 3.30 – 4.30pm

In the School Gym

with

Mr Pownall

EVERYBODY WELCOME

"Brilliant!" I yelled, and ran to join the others back in Mrs Weaver's classroom.

"I don't know what *you're* so excited about, Frogface," sneered Ryan Scott, who had followed me in. "Mr Pownall doesn't want soppy girls trying to play football. It's a boys' game. You'd just be wasting your time if you turned up."

"I know you can't read, Spotty Scotty," I snapped back at him, "so I'd better tell you that Mr Pownall has written 'everyone welcome' and underlined '*everyone*'. So he must mean that he doesn't mind if no-talent wasters like you turn up. And he'll certainly be pleased to see talent like mine – whether I'm a girl or not."

"Yeah, right McKenzie, in your dreams!"

"Ryan Scott, why are you always the last one to find your place?" Mrs Weaver suddenly appeared. "Is there something wrong with your chair? Does it bring you out in a rash? Please enlighten me."

Ryan Scott blushed beetroot red and sat down. But not before he'd given me a really filthy look. I love it when he gets told off like that, he just can't handle it.

When we'd all settled down to some maths, Frankie whispered to me:

"I think Scotty's probably right, you know. I bet Mr Pownall doesn't really expect any girls to turn up to his five-a-side practice."

"Well, he's going to be surprised then," I told her with a grin, "because I'm definitely going."

"You'll only embarrass yourself," warned Fliss from the other side of the table.

"And whose side are you on?" I asked. "As if I couldn't guess." I started to chant, "Felicity loves Ryan, Felicity loves Ryan!"

"Shut up!" hissed Fliss. It was her turn to do an impression of a beetroot. She and Ryan Scott certainly have a lot in common!

"Laura McKenzie!" Mrs Weaver said sharply. "I hope there's a very good excuse for your outburst."

"Sorry, I just got a bit carried away," I apologised. "Maths always does that to me. I must be allergic to it!"

"This allergic reaction probably explains why your maths book is always in such a mess," said Mrs Weaver crisply. "I think the cure for your complaint is extra maths homework. I think you'll soon find that you're not allergic to it any more. Would you like to try that?"

Mrs Weaver was looking at me and everyone else was falling about laughing.

"Actually, I'm feeling a lot better now, thank you," I mumbled.

After that I kept my head down and got on with my work. I thought that if Mrs Weaver caught me talking again she just might carry out her threat and I couldn't face that. I nearly cracked when Ryan Scott started flicking bits of rubber at me though. He was dying to get me into trouble and I was dying to bop him one. But I didn't. I kept cool and promised myself that I'd teach him a lesson at the five-a-side practice.

It was quite a relief to get outside at break time. I did a few cartwheels on the grass next to our classroom, then went to join the others.

They were all standing around watching Ryan Scott kicking a ball about with his mates.

"Aw, come on, we could do better than that!" I moaned. "They're useless."

"They look pretty good to me!" said Rosie.

"All right then," I reasoned, "if you come to the five-a-side practice you'll soon be good enough to join in with them."

"Uurgh, we wouldn't want to!" Frankie shuddered. "I couldn't think of anything worse. Stupid football AND horrible boys. *Gross!*"

Frankie just wasn't being reasonable, but I wasn't giving up yet.

"*You* wouldn't mind spending more time with the boys at the practice, would you Fliss?" I asked. She was going all moony-eyed looking at stupid Ryan Scott.

"Leave it out Kenny!" she snapped. "I can't play football and everybody would laugh at me. I have enough of that with you lot!"

"Ah, diddums!" we all yelled, and grabbed her so hard in one of our group bear hugs that soon she was squealing for mercy!

"What about you, Lyndz?" I asked when we

finally let Fliss go. "You'll come to the practice won't you? It'll be fun, honest!"

Lyndz didn't look too sure about that.

"I don't think so Kenny," she replied. "I promised Mrs McAllister that I'd go down to the stables after school on Wednesday. She's got a show the next day and I said I'd help to groom the horses."

"You and your horses!" I grumbled. I'd kind of been banking on Lyndz coming with me.

"Hey, what about you, Rosie?" I then asked. "You're good at sports. Wouldn't you love to show those boys that we're just as good as them?"

"Well, yes," said Rosie slowly.

"Thanks Rosie, my great mate!" I slapped her on the back. "I knew that you wouldn't let me down!" I scowled at the others, especially Frankie.

"Hang on a minute, Kenny," said Rosie. "I only said that I'd like to teach the boys a lesson. I don't think I'll be doing that at the five-a-side practice though."

"What do you mean?" I yelled.

"Look, it's all right for you," Rosie explained. "You're always playing football, so you know what it's all about. We don't. I can't even kick a ball for my dog. The last thing we want is to show ourselves up in front of Ryan Scott and his stupid mates. They'll never let us forget it. I'm afraid you're on your own on this one. Sorry!"

I couldn't *believe* it. My so-called friends were all going to let me down.

The whistle blew and the others ran inside. It was our turn to choose books from the library and they were all excited about which ones they were going to borrow. But I couldn't stop thinking about the practice on Wednesday. It felt a bit funny knowing that I'd be going on my own. Don't get me wrong, I wasn't scared or anything. I do tons of stuff by myself outside school. It's just that we usually do school-based activities all together. It would have been a laugh having the others there, that's all. As it was, it looked as though I would have to stand up for Girl Power on the football pitch all by myself!

CHAPTER TWO

I didn't exactly give up hope about the others coming to the practice with me, but by Wednesday afternoon I knew for sure that I'd be going by myself. I'd spent all of Tuesday and most of Wednesday morning trying to persuade them to come along – but no joy. I mean, what does a girl have to do to get a bit of support from her friends?

I tried threatening them by saying that if they didn't come with me I'd never speak to them again.

"Sounds like a great idea to me!" laughed Frankie. "What do you think, Lyndz?"

Lyndz giggled and said, "You bet!" so that didn't work.

"What about if I buy you all loads of sweets?" I asked.

"You?" shrieked Rosie. "You've never got any money! What do you plan on buying them with? Buttons?"

Hmm, I guess I hadn't thought that through either.

"All right then," I told them. "If you don't come with me, I'll put up a poster saying how much Fliss is in love with Ryan Scott."

Frankie just said, "Like everybody doesn't already know!"

Fliss meanwhile blushed and went all silly and giggly. If you ask me, she actually *wanted* me to put up a poster. That girl has a serious problem!

Well, after that it was no surprise when the clock hit 3.30pm that the others all went home giggling and shouting, "Bye Kenny, have fun!"

And I headed for the gym – alone.

*　　*　　*

19

I went in to the girls' changing rooms first and pulled from my bag my trackie bottoms and my favourite Leicester City football shirt. I couldn't wait to take off my stupid school uniform. I *hate* it. It's the only time that I EVER wear a skirt. I'm sure that I'd work much better if I could wear what I wanted at school. I'd probably even be able to do maths. But I guess if Fliss could wear what she wanted, she'd never get to school in the first place because she'd be dithering between her mini-skirts and her bootlegs. Then of course school would turn into one big fashion show. Maybe uniforms aren't such a bad idea after all. But I still think girls should be allowed to wear trousers if we want to.

I was thinking about the school uniform thing the whole time I was getting changed. And let's face it, I had plenty of time because no-one else came in to disturb me. But by the time I'd pulled on my trainers, I didn't really care. I'd got myself all pumped up and I was ready to face Ryan Scott and his stupid cronies.

When I got out into the gym, everything looked different. A new pitch had been marked out in the middle and there were a titchy pair of goals at either end. I knew it must be a five-a-side pitch so I went to investigate.

"It's Laura McKenzie isn't it?" a voice suddenly boomed behind me. I spun round so quickly I went all dizzy. The voice belonged to Mr Pownall. He must have come into the gym when I wasn't looking.

"Th… that's right!" I stuttered.

"I wondered if you'd be coming along to my five-a-side practices, Laura," Mr Pownall continued. "I've heard how much you like football. It's good to see you!"

I smiled at him, but there was something that I just had to put right. I was going to feel really stupid in front of the boys if he went around calling me Laura all the time.

"Actually, I hate being called Laura," I told him. "My friends all call me Kenny."

"Right, Kenny it is," smiled Mr Pownall. "Ah, here come the rest of our happy band. For a moment then I thought we might have to devise a new game: one-a-side football!"

There was a great clatter as the doors from the boys' changing room burst open and Ryan Scott and Danny McCloud stalked across the gym. They were pretending to be Gladiators. Pathetic! They were followed by a group of younger boys who were all looking at Ryan Scott as though he was Alan Shearer or something. I mean, come on! The boy looks more like Chuckie from Rugrats!

As soon as Ryan Scott saw me he asked angrily, "What's *she* doing here?"

"I've come to show you a thing or two about football!" I snapped back.

"Yeah, right!" sneered Scotty-chops. "Don't you think we should see if she knows how to kick the ball, sir? She's only going to slow us down if she can't, and that wouldn't be fair!"

(You see – Ryan Scott and Fliss do have a lot in common! Fliss is always going on about things being 'fair'.)

Before Mr Pownall could answer, Danny McCloud had tossed a football towards me.

"I'll show them!" I told myself, and started

heading the ball, keeping it up in the air as long as I could. Then I took it on my knee and bounced it from one knee to the other without letting it touch the ground. Then – and this is the clever bit – I trapped the ball on my foot and flicked it on to my knee and kept doing that until Ryan Scott got so mad that he snatched the ball away from me. The others kids broke into applause, and old Scotty looked so mad I thought he might explode.

"That's easy to do!" he snapped. "I bet you can't pass it properly though, can you?"

I was just about to prove that my passing skills were as deadly as David Beckham's, when Mr Pownall grabbed the football.

"That was very impressive Kenny," he said. "But I'm afraid heading skills won't be of any use to you in five-a-side football."

We all looked blankly at him.

"You see this really is a game of FOOTball. If anyone kicks the ball over head height, it automatically means that a free kick is awarded to the other team."

I must admit that I'd always thought that

five-a-side football was exactly the same as the eleven-a-side variety, but with fewer people on the team obviously. WRONG! Mr Pownall explained that it's a different game entirely.

"When the ball goes over the touchline, a player from the other team doesn't THROW it in, they have to ROLL it in," he explained. "And corners are rolled in too."

"But you do score the same, don't you sir?" asked Danny McCloud, who was beginning to look a bit confused.

"Well, yes and no," replied Mr Pownall. "The object of the game is still to get the ball in the back of the net, but you can only score from outside the area. There are no delicate tap-ins with five-a-side!"

We'd been standing around quite a bit, and I think Mr Pownall sensed that we were eager to get on and play.

"Right we'll discuss the rules of the game as we go along. Let's get warmed up first!" he said.

We jogged round, and when we were warm enough we stretched out. Then Mr Pownall divided us into groups. He lined up some cones, and first we had to run through them and back to our team, then we had to dribble a ball through them. Ryan Scott was in my team, worse luck, so he never stopped trying to wind me up.

"You think you're so clever, don't you?" he muttered when I was waiting for my turn. "Beginners' luck! Just wait until we play a *proper* game – then you'll see how it's really done!"

"Yeah right!" I hissed back. "Like I'll be impressed by *you*! I've seen you playing football in the playground, don't forget. I've seen better skills from my mate's dog!"

Ryan Scott was not a happy boy! I think Mr Pownall sensed that we weren't exactly the best of friends, so he made us all swap teams for the next exercises and made sure that Ryan and I were on different ones. Actually, that was cool because it meant that we were racing against each other. We did this thing where you had to dribble the ball around various obstacles, then shoot at goal. I'm so used to doing that kind of thing in the garden that it was a piece of cake and I scored every time. Old Scotty kept getting freaked when he saw me and shot his ball over the goal every time. It caught Mr Pownall right in the face once which was kind of funny, although we didn't know whether we should laugh or not.

Danny McCloud was on my team, and you could tell that he was kind of impressed by the way I could play football. Although of course he's a boy, so he found it really hard to admit it. It was only when our team came first in all the exercises that he got a bit carried away and said: "Hey McKenzie you're quite good!" before adding, "… for a girl!"

The time just whizzed past. I couldn't believe it when Mr Pownall said that the hour was almost up. We just had ten minutes left, and he said that we could have a go at playing a proper five-a-side game, just to get the feel of it. There were nine of us at the practice so he said that he'd make up the numbers.

"Right Kenny and Ryan, you can pick the teams. You first, Kenny."

I love picking teams. I looked at the faces in front of me, all looking eager – and desperate not to be the one left until the end. But you'll never guess who was looking most eager of all and jumping around going:

"Kenny, pick me, pick me!"

Danny McCloud, that's who! I mean, that's not cool from someone of his age, now is it? But still, I felt kind of chuffed. I mean, he wanted to come on my team rather than on his best mate Ryan's! I would have picked him anyway just to wind old Scotty-chops up. But he actually *wanted* to be on my team. Boy, did Ryan look MAD!

After we'd picked the teams we didn't have time for much of a game. But I did have time to do this blinding run, skipping over a tackle from Scotty before passing the ball to Danny who shot it into the back of the net. Usually in that situation I'd go ballistic and do some crazy celebration. But this time was different. I mean, did I really want to fling my arms around Danny McCloud in order to celebrate the goal? I think not! That's when it hit me that

27

this school five-a-side thing with only boys for company might have a few drawbacks. I really had to get my mates interested. But that was going to be easier said than done – as I was about to find out!

CHAPTER THREE

After that first five-a-side football practice, everything suddenly got very complicated. You see, I was suddenly in demand! You could have knocked me down with a feather when as soon as I got into the playground on Thursday morning, Danny McCloud shouted out:

"Oi, McKenzie! Fancy a game?"

He was holding up a football and was with a couple of the other guys in our class.

Now, that kind of thing doesn't happen every day. I know that boys would never say it straight out, but this was like them admitting that they thought I was good at football.

I did look round to see if Frankie or the others were there before I joined in, I really did. But they weren't. So of course I went over to play footie. *Bad move!* The others went ballistic with me when I finally caught up with them in the classroom.

"We *always* meet up before the start of school," Fliss kept whingeing, like I'd just poisoned her goldfish or something.

"I expect you'll be dropping us at break times now as well!" sniffed Frankie as soon as I'd sat down.

"Yeah, and playing with your new boyfriends," added Rosie.

"They are *not* my boyfriends," I told them angrily.

And to be honest, I didn't think I'd be asked to play with the boys again anyway, because when Ryan Scott had turned up he didn't exactly seem thrilled that I was playing football with his mates.

Sure enough, when lunchtime came, all the boys went to play football and walked past me as though I wasn't even there. Except for Danny

McCloud. He just shrugged his shoulders like he was apologising or something.

"Looks like they were just using you after all!" sneered Fliss with a told-you-so smirk plastered all over her face.

"Well, maybe I was using *them* to kill time until you lot turned up!" I snapped back at her.

"You didn't exactly notice us when we did appear!" moaned Rosie.

"Yeah, well, I'm sorry about that. You know what it's like when you're busy playing something."

"You mean you'd rather play with the boys than play with us!" Fliss exploded. "Well that's charming, isn't it?"

"Shut up for goodness sake!" I yelled. "They were playing football and I just happened to join in. That's not a crime, is it?"

"Oooh, get her!" the others piped up.

"Chill out Kenny, for goodness sake!" laughed Frankie.

"Yeah, chill out!" shrieked Lyndz and Rosie together. They ran up behind me and started to tickle me all over. In seconds I was writhing in a heap on the ground with tears streaming down my face.

"I'm going to get you for this!" I eventually managed to gasp.

"Oh yeah?" giggled Rosie. "Prove it."

I struggled up from the ground and managed to grab hold of Fliss. I bundled into her and started barging her over to the grass outside our classroom. She was dead scared at first, you could tell, but then she realised I was playing one of our Gladiator games and started to barge me back. Just when I thought I'd got the upper hand, Frankie grabbed hold of my arm. She spun me round faster and faster like one of those crazy fairground rides. It was *wicked*! When our legs finally gave way we collapsed in a heap on the ground.

"Now come on Kenny, admit it!" she gasped when she'd got her breath back. "You have much more fun with us than with some stupid boys, don't you?"

"Yeah, sure!" I agreed, but inside I was still feeling kind of annoyed. I mean, I was getting all this earache about one little kick-around. It was like the others thought they owned me or something. And besides, if they'd bothered to come along to the five-a-side practice with me in the first place, they could have joined in with the footie too. Then they might not have been so jealous.

I was still feeling pretty annoyed with them by afternoon break. So when Danny McCloud came over and asked if I wanted to join in their football game, I leapt at the chance. You ought to have seen the others' faces. I swear that Fliss could have swallowed a bus, her mouth was so wide open. Ryan Scott wasn't too thrilled about it either, but one of the other boys had had to go home with a bad stomach ache so he really didn't have much choice.

It was well cool. You see, it was great to be actually playing football with someone. Usually I have to practice my skills by myself in the garden. Molly the Monster, my stupid sister, wouldn't be seen dead playing football. Neither would Emma my eldest sister, and Mum and Dad are just too busy.

I had a great time. Even Ryan Scott wasn't

too bad after a while. He's a totally different person when he's playing football – he's almost normal. But of course my friends weren't happy at *all*. They kept trying to make out that if I liked them so much I shouldn't really need to play football as well. Crazy.

Anyway, from then on I tried a sort of compromise. I played football with the boys during morning and afternoon breaks, and stayed with my mates at lunchtime. But they were still mad at me. Especially as the more I played football and the more I went to the five-a-side practices, the more I found that I was sharing jokes with the boys in class. And of course the others couldn't join in. I felt bad, I really did, but I must admit that I was enjoying myself too. I know that it's not going to sound too good admitting this, but it felt great to be so popular with the boys. I could more than hold my own in their rough games and they sort of respected me for that. I think they accepted me as one of them, which was great because any of my friends will tell you what a tomboy I am.

But still, the others just couldn't understand me at all. Even Lyndz had a go at me, and you know how calm she usually is.

"You just don't care about the Sleepover Club any more, do you?" she tackled me one afternoon after school. "You're so busy playing football with those stupid boys, it's like we don't even exist any more."

"Don't be daft, Lyndz!" I tried to reassure her. "Playing football with the guys is different. Besides, I don't see why I can't have other friends too. We don't complain when you're at the stables all the time, do we?"

"That's different," she said defensively. "That's after school. Besides, you see Ryan Scott and Danny McCloud more than you see us now."

Thinking about it she was probably right. As well as playing football with them in the breaks, I sometimes stayed behind after school to play with them. So I didn't walk home with the others as much as I used to. I told you that things got a bit complicated, didn't I?

Those five-a-side practices certainly had a lot to answer for. But they were *great*. By the second week we really started to get the hang of it. We still kept forgetting about some of the rules, like not kicking the ball over head height, so Mr Pownall had to blow his whistle every ten seconds to award a free kick. It was hysterical. And during one game he awarded ten penalties because the goalkeepers – Alex Brown and Neil Hughes – kept forgetting that they couldn't leave their areas. The rest of us just creased up about that. But at least we were learning the rules as we went along.

That definitely proved to be a good thing, because after about three weeks or so, Mr Pownall called us all together at the end of the practice and announced that there was going to be a five-a-side competition in the area.

"Now I know that you haven't been playing this very long, but it would be great if we could enter at least one team in the competition," he told us.

"Yeaah!"

"All right!"

Everyone seemed to be leaping around and punching the air. I was yelling louder than anyone. This could be my big chance. Some big football scout might spot my talent and train me to be the first female professional footballer in Britain. I was definitely up for it.

The only thing that worried me was the extra practice I'd have to do if I was going to make the team. Extra practice would of course mean spending more time with the boys. And we all knew what *that* would mean. Yup – trouble from Frankie and the others. But I thought they would understand how much a place in the team would mean to me, I really did. But I was wrong about that too. *Very* wrong.

"So you're finally going to choose them over us, are you?" demanded Frankie when I tried to explain things to her in the playground the next morning.

"It's not like that," I explained. "It's not a case of choosing. I need the boys to practise with, that's all. Once the competition's over, I won't play with them so much. I promise."

The others looked at each other.

"We don't believe you," said Fliss coldly.

"Believe what you like," I snapped.

"It seems like we're not enough fun for you any more," said Lyndz sadly. "You don't like playing with us, do you?"

"Yes I do! It's just that I like playing football, and you don't play do you?"

The gang all stared at each other with these really weird looks on their faces.

"What's up with you?" I demanded.

"If football's *that* important to you, I don't really think we have that much in common, do we?" asked Frankie. Her voice sounded cold, but when I looked at her, her eyes were really sad.

"Yes we do!" I didn't want Frankie getting upset. We'd been best mates for ever.

"But if we asked you to choose between us and football, you'd choose football, right?" demanded Rosie.

That was a tough one.

"I don't know," I admitted. "It's just that this competition is kind of important to me right now. When it's over, everything will be back to normal, you'll see."

It was the answer that they didn't want, but I guess it was the one that they'd expected to hear. They just sort of shrugged and turned away from me, just like that. I'll never forget the way that felt. Even when Danny called me over for a game of footie, I felt kind of lonely and a bit empty inside.

CHAPTER FOUR

Now I know what you're thinking. You're thinking that the Sleepover Club broke up then and there over my football, right? Well we didn't, not really. I mean, we still hung round together – it's just things were a bit strained. I didn't spend time with my mates like I used to, and when I *did* see them, they always seemed to be planning things together which didn't include me. But that didn't really matter because I was spending all my time practising for the trials for our five-a-side team anyway. Mr Pownall had announced that they would take place on September 15th, and he'd put up a notice inviting anyone who was interested to watch.

I'd tried to be really good when I was with the others and not mention football at all. It just wasn't worth the aggro. But on the days running up to the trial I was so hyper I just couldn't help myself.

"You *will* be coming to watch the five-a-side trials, won't you?" I asked them on Monday afternoon in our craft lesson. We were up to our elbows in papier-mâché, and Fliss was trying hard to pretend that she was enjoying it. She *hates* getting her hands dirty.

They exchanged glances and looked all embarrassed.

"Well actually, we've planned to go rollerblading in the park after school on Wednesday," explained Frankie quietly.

Rollerblading! They never used to do that.

"How long have you been rollerblading?" I asked, trying not to sound annoyed that they hadn't told me about it.

"A few weeks now," gushed Fliss. "It's well cool. I was terrified at first and I kept falling

41

over but the others helped me and now…"

I don't know what she went twittering on about because I stopped listening. I couldn't believe that they'd do something like that without me.

Suddenly I felt someone nudging me.

"Kenny… Kenny, are you all right?"

"What? Sorry, yes."

"You don't mind if we don't come to watch do you?" Frankie asked.

"No, that's cool," I lied. "Have a good time."

I must admit that after that I went round in a bit of a fog. I realised how much I missed being with the others. And I didn't have anyone to talk to any more. Frankie and I always used to ring each other up if anything was bugging us, but now I figured Frankie wouldn't want to listen to my problems – especially as they involved her. Besides, I hated to admit that I might have made a mistake in choosing football over my friends. Still, as football seemed to be about all I was left with, I just had to make sure that I got into the five-a-side team.

By the time Wednesday afternoon came round I was a bag of nerves. As I was leaving for the gym, the others stopped me.

"Good luck!" said Rosie and Fliss together.

"Hope you make the team!" smiled Frankie.

"I'm sure you will." Lyndz gave me a reassuring squeeze of my arm.

I felt a bit choked to be honest, but I didn't let them see that. I just said, "Thanks, I'll do my best," and headed for the gym.

As soon as I was changed I went into the gym, expecting the usual boys and maybe a few of their friends to be there. I couldn't believe how many people there were! It looked like some of the guys had brought along their entire families – including the cat! (No, that's not quite true. Ryan Scott's dog *was* there, but Mr Pownall made his brother take it home when it started weeing over some of the equipment.) Looking round at all those people, I kind of wished that I'd asked someone along to watch me. Even Molly the Monster would have been better than nobody.

"Ah, Kenny." Mr Pownall ran over to me. He

looked a bit flustered. I guess he hadn't expected so many people to turn up either. "There's something I've got to…"

I'm afraid I didn't hear what he said next because out of the corner of my eye I noticed some more people entering the gym. I was sure that I recognised that coat, and that hairstyle – and those hiccups.

"*You came!*" I flew over to where Frankie, Rosie, Lyndz and Fliss were standing.

"Boy am I glad you're here!" I told them. "I thought I was going to have no-one cheering me on."

"What makes you think we're here to see you?" asked Fliss, eyeing up Ryan Scott.

Frankie must have seen my face fall. "She's only joking, idiot!" she laughed, punching me on the arm. "We wouldn't have missed it."

"Look, I'm really sorry that I've been a bit of a dipstick lately," I muttered.

"Hey, hic, forget it," smiled Lyndz.

"Look, you'd better be going," said Rosie. "Mr Pownall seems to be calling everyone together."

"See you later!" I called as I ran to the other end of the gym.

"Break a leg!" shouted Fliss.

I turned to see the others shoving her and telling her to be quiet.

"Ow!" Fliss was squealing. "I thought that's what you're supposed to say…"

Some things never change!

It's funny how five minutes can change the way you're feeling. When I joined the rest of the guys who were trying out for the team, I wasn't panicking any more. In fact I felt really positive and confident. Mr Pownall explained that we'd be doing our usual training exercises and then playing a full game. He said that he'd be watching us all closely and at the end of the hour he'd be announcing who he had picked for the team. I couldn't wait to get on with it.

"Kenny," he called me towards him. "I don't know if you were listening earlier, but you do know that…"

THWACK! A ball landed smack in my left ear. It didn't half hurt. I turned round and saw Ryan

Scott smirking like anything.

"Sorry," he said, not looking sorry at all. "It was an accident, honest."

"Well just be more careful in future!" Mr Pownall told him crossly.

I was *furious*. I bet Scotty-chops was trying to knock me out or something, just so I wouldn't be in the team. Well, it was going to take more than that to stop me.

I got the ball and dribbled it past Ryan, calling, "Come on then, get it off me!"

Mr Pownall shouted, "Kenny... Kenny... Oh, I'll tell you later!"

Then he blew his whistle and we started on the exercises.

I know that I shouldn't say this, but they were really quite easy. I mean, it was the same stuff we do every week, so it shouldn't have been a surprise to anyone. But the way some of the boys played, you'd think they'd never even *seen* a football in their lives before. I mean, they were just so BAD! Even Danny McCloud seemed to be put off by all the noise the spectators were making, and that's just stupid. Have you ever seen a professional footballer go to pieces in front of a big crowd? Of course not, they love all the attention – and so do I! I played the best I'd ever played in my life. It really helped when I looked across and Frankie, Lyndz and Rosie were going wild with their cheering. Even Fliss looked as though she was letting her hair down – a tiny bit!

When it came to the actual match I was on *fire*. I mean, I was just so hot I couldn't put a foot wrong. Danny, Ryan and I were on the same team and all our practising together really paid off. We could sort of tell where the other person was going to pass the ball; it was like telepathy or something. We played a blinder, and by half-time (which in five-a-side matches is after six minutes) we were three–nil up and we'd each scored a goal.

"We're all bound to get in the team at this rate," Danny said as we were changing ends. "And if we play like this in the competition, I can't see anyone beating us, can you?"

Scotty and I had to admit that we did appear pretty invincible.

The second half got even better. Neil Hughes in the opposite goal let his brain go walkabout again and kept handling the ball outside his area. We were awarded four penalties. We had this arrangement before the match that we'd take it in turns to shoot penalties. The other boy on our team, David Harper, said he wasn't bothered. I think he was a bit intimidated by us actually. Anyway, I ended up taking two of our penalties. What do you mean, did I score? Of *course* I did! Scotty-chops missed his though, which was a shame. No, I genuinely felt sorry for him about that.

By the end of the match, the score was 7–2 to our team. We'd played out of our socks, and we were as high as kites when Mr Pownall called us all over to announce the team. The gym had been going wild, but as soon as Mr Pownall said that he was ready to make his announcement it went deadly quiet.

"In goal, we'll have Alex Brown…"

We commiserated with Neil Hughes and told him "better luck next time".

My heart began to thump and I prepared

myself for hearing my name next.

"The rest of the team will be Ryan Scott, Danny McCloud, Bobby Brook and…"

My name had to be next, it just *had* to be. I could hear Frankie and the others chanting "Kenny, Kenny, Kenny!"

"… Charlie Acres. And the reserves will be…"

I couldn't believe it. I was better than all the others on the pitch and he hadn't even picked me to be in the team. I wasn't sure that I wanted to be a reserve.

"… Dean Sullivan and Michael Blackwell."

I wasn't even down as a *reserve*! What had I done wrong?

It was Ryan Scott who piped up first.

"But what about McKenzie, sir?"

"Yeah, she's the best player here," agreed Danny. "After me and Ryan of course!"

Frankie, Fliss, Lyndz and Rosie came flying over. "Why haven't you picked Kenny?" they demanded. "She played a blinder."

Mr Pownall held up his hands to silence everybody.

"I tried to tell Kenny before the trials, but she didn't listen to me," he explained.

I looked at him blankly.

"I couldn't pick you because girls aren't allowed to play in a boys' team. No mixed teams are allowed. It's the rule. I really am sorry, Kenny." He sounded quite upset himself. "If you can find enough girls to form your own team, then you can enter the competition. What about that?"

He was smiling at me but I had to turn away. I could feel big tears welling up in my eyes and I wasn't going to let anyone see me cry.

"I'm really sorry, Kenny," Danny McCloud mumbled as he walked past me.

"Kenny, I don't believe it! You were brilliant out there!" Frankie grabbed me and gave me a big hug.

"Yeah better than the boys – by miles!" agreed Rosie.

"Well it doesn't matter now does it," I muttered, "because I'm a girl and it doesn't matter how well I can play."

I headed for the changing room, where I'd left my bag.

"Don't be like that," said Frankie when she caught up with me. "You heard what Mr Pownall said. All you need to do is find some other girls who can play football, and then you can enter the competition too."

"And where am I going to find four girls who can make up the rest of my team?" I asked. "They don't exactly grow on trees, you know."

I put my head in my hands. I'd dreamed and dreamed of playing in that competition, and now it had been snatched away from me. I glanced up and the others were all looking at me full of concern.

"Hang on a minute!" I shrieked, suddenly coming to life. "There are four of you! We could start our very own five-a-side team!"

"Oh no!" laughed Frankie, shaking her head. "No way!"

CHAPTER FIVE

You didn't think I'd let them get away so easily, did you? Of course I didn't! Once I have a plan in my head, nothing, but *nothing*, will make me give up on it. Especially where football is concerned. But at the same time I knew that I had to tread pretty carefully. Football had just nearly split us up after all – the last thing my friends needed was me ramming it down their throats again. So I decided to play it cool.

"Sorry guys," I apologised. "I know that football's not your thing. It was silly of me to even think we could form a team. Forget I even mentioned it."

"Don't worry, we will!" sniffed Fliss.

But at least Lyndz and Rosie looked as though they might just be giving it some thought. I don't know what Frankie was thinking – she's hard to figure out sometimes.

When I'd changed, we all sneaked out of the back of the gym so that I wouldn't have to face Ryan Scott and the others.

"At least you've got us!" Frankie whispered, squeezing my arm.

Yes, but did that mean that they were prepared to drop everything to form a five-a-side team? Somehow I doubted it. But I was convinced that all it needed was some of my famous McKenzie persuasion, and soon they'd be *begging* to play football in the competition with me. What I needed was a plan!

I mulled it over all evening, and by the next morning I knew exactly what I had to do. But first I had to face the boys.

"Come on Kenny, we're waiting for you!" shouted Danny McCloud as soon as I got into the playground.

"Nah, I think I'll give it a miss, thanks," I called back.

He just shrugged his shoulders.

"I never thought I'd see you passing up the chance to play football," Frankie shouted as she ran towards me.

"There's not much point now, is there?" I muttered sadly.

"That's a silly attitude," she warned me firmly. "You can't give up on something just like that."

"Well, unless I miraculously turn into a boy overnight, I don't see how I'm going to play in the competition, do you?"

"You could disguise yourself," she suggested.

"Get real, Frankie!" I laughed. "You've been watching too many films."

The others soon joined us. But Fliss might as well have been on Mars for all the attention she gave us. She was too busy watching Ryan Scott playing football. Does that girl need a brain transplant or what? But it did present me with an ideal opportunity to put Phase One of my plan into action.

"He's pretty good, isn't he?" I asked, going to stand with her. "He's actually quite nice too, once he's playing football. There's a whole different side to him that you've never seen."

"Really?"

"Yeah, but you only ever see it when you're playing football with him," I told her seriously.

"I bet he's still annoying though, isn't he?" asked Rosie, who had joined us.

"Only some of the time!" I laughed. "On the football pitch he actually listened to what I had to say for once. I had this amazing feeling of power over the boys when they realised that I had more idea about tactics than they did."

My plan certainly seemed to be working, because Fliss and Rosie were still chatting together about boys and football when the bell went.

I didn't have to wait too long before I could put Phase Two into operation: our next netball practice on Friday, to be precise. We all got there early, and I just happened to get my hands on a ball before Miss Burnie, the

55

teacher, appeared. I started kicking it about and soon the others joined in. Every time Lyndz took a shot I yelled, "Great shot Lyndz!" or "I wish I could do that!"

Lyndz looked chuffed to bits, and you could tell that she was getting more confident too.

"Girls! If you want to play football I suggest that you find Mr Pownall. This is a netball court!" Trust Miss Burnie to spoil our fun.

"You really are good at football!" I told Lyndz as we were waiting for the netball practice to start. "You should play more, you know. You'd run rings round the boys."

"I don't think so!" Lyndz said, blushing. "My brothers all laugh at me when I try to play with them."

"Well, they're just jealous," I told her confidently. "Just think if you did play, it would be like proving to your brothers that they're wrong about you. I bet they'd take you more seriously too."

Well, that *really* got Lyndz thinking, you could tell. Now all I had to do was work on Frankie.

Actually, as it turned out, Frankie was smarter than I'd figured. She came up to me one lunchtime the following week, after I'd been telling Fliss how much Ryan Scott admired sporty girls.

"He says that they're much more fun," I told her. "Look how well I got on with him after the five-a-side practices."

I could see that she was getting pretty jealous.

"If *you* turned up at one of those practices, you'd knock his socks off for sure!" I reassured her. "Ow!"

Frankie very rudely interrupted me by nipping my arm and dragging me off to a corner of the playground.

"I know what you're doing," she hissed, "and I'm not sure that it's going to work."

"What do you mean?" I asked, all innocent.

"You're trying to force us all to form a five-a-side team for the competition, aren't you?" she asked menacingly.

"Might be."

"Look Kenny, we know how much the

competition means to you, and I for one would love to help out," she went on. "But we're not going to make fools of ourselves for you or for anybody."

"You won't!" I promised. "All we need is some practice."

"Even Fliss?" asked Frankie. "She's not exactly Alan Shearer, is she? Neither is Rosie, come to that."

"Well one of them can go in goal," I reasoned. "And between you, me and Lyndz we should be able to pull it off. Thanks, Frankie – you're the greatest!"

"Talk about twisting my arm!" laughed Frankie. "OK then, I'll help, but haven't you forgotten something? We've still got to persuade the others what a brilliant idea this is, remember? And another thing McKenzie," she added in her best gangster's voice, "if this comes off, you owe me. Big time!"

All week I kicked a football around whenever I got the chance, and Frankie always joined in. Sure enough, after a few minutes the others joined in too, and we had a right laugh. So what if Fliss kept missing the ball, or Rosie kept tripping up? They were having a good time. Whenever any of the boys appeared, we pretended we'd just found the ball and were mucking about with it. The last thing I needed was those stupid idiots making fun of us – that would put Fliss and Rosie off for life.

"You know what we need?" I asked the others on the Wednesday. "A football-themed sleepover, that's what!"

"Why?" asked Rosie and Fliss together. "We've never had one before."

Frankie and I looked at each other.

"That's precisely why," Frankie burst in quickly. "We've never had one and it would be kind of different. Remember that great horse-themed one we had? That was fun, wasn't it?"

Everybody started giggling about the clothes and the games, not to mention the food we'd had at our horsey sleepover.

"So is everybody agreed that a football sleepover is a good plan?" I shouted.

"Yes!"

"Right, my place, Saturday. Be there or be a banana!" I laughed, throwing a load of invitations at everyone. It had taken me ages to write them all the night before, and it had taken me even longer to bribe Molly the Monster into letting me have our bedroom without her poking her nose in every five minutes. (I did threaten to leave my rat Merlin in her bed one night, but she said that I was disgusting and that she'd tell Mum. So in the end I had to promise to buy her a bag of crisps every day for a week. What a creep!)

Anyway, I've got a spare copy of the invitation here. What do you think? Cool eh?

Kenny is having a
FOOTBALL SLEEPOVER
On Saturday 25th September
Wear togs to play football in
Bring 'football-type' food
for the Midnight Feast!
Party on, dudes!

So at least everybody knew what to expect at the sleepover – it wasn't as though I'd conned them or anything. It's just that I hadn't exactly told them that they would be forming our five-a-side team either. But hey, it was my job to show them how great it would be, and Frankie had promised that she would help.

It all started out well enough. Saturday was a really warm sunny day, so I'd set up loads of stuff in the garden. Everybody knows that I'm a bit wild and I like to let off as much steam as possible. In fact I was charging about like a mad monkey when everyone appeared.

"So what exactly has that got to do with football?" asked Frankie as soon as she saw me. "I know that some players act like animals, but that's ridiculous!"

"Ha ha ha!" I laughed. "Hey you all look wicked. Let's have a look at you!"

Fliss paraded about in the new tiny white shorts and stripy top she'd got for her birthday. It's true that I'd never seen a footballer wearing make-up and plaits before, but at least Fliss had entered into the spirit of things.

"I've brought my tracksuit in case it gets cold," she explained. "I really wanted to show you my new skirt though. I mean, this isn't really *me*, is it?"

"You look fab!" I gushed. "If only Ryan Scott could see you now!"

Frankie shot me a warning glance. We'd agreed that we wouldn't mention the actual competition until everyone was chilling out – probably when we were having our midnight feast.

"If you tell them too early everyone will freak out and the sleepover will be a disaster," she had warned me.

I thought that Frankie was wrong about that, but I didn't say anything else to Fliss all the same. Instead I turned my attention to the others. When I saw Rosie I didn't really know what to think.

"What are you like!" I gasped when I saw her. She was wearing this mega-long pair of baggy shorts and a really thick long shirt.

"It's what my grandad used to play football in," she explained. "Mum found it in a box in the attic. What do you think?" She pretended to do a catwalk turn.

"I bet Ryan Scott wouldn't fancy you if he saw you in that!" sniffed Fliss.

"I wouldn't want him to," Rosie snapped right back. "I only came in this as a joke. I wish I hadn't bothered."

"Don't be daft, you look great!" Frankie laughed. "Too great!" She grabbed Rosie and wrestled her to the floor. The rest of us piled on top.

"We've got to make those clothes a bit dirtier so you all look like proper footballers," I squealed, making sure that Rosie and Fliss got the dirtiest of all of us.

"I thought you were going to be playing football!" Dad suddenly appeared on the patio. "That looks more like a rugby scrum to me!"

We all scrambled up from the ground.

"We're just getting into the swing of things," I explained. He looks a bit straight, my dad, but he's kind of cool really.

"So I see," he smiled. "Well it's good to see the rest of you girls. And it's really good of you to help Kenny get over her disappointment with that five-a-side thing like this. I'm sure you'll be splendid when you form your…"

"Thanks Dad," I butted in quickly. "I think Mum's calling for you."

"I didn't hear… oh, right, I can take a hint!" Dad disappeared inside again.

"What did your dad mean, Kenny?" Lyndz was looking very suspicious. "How are we helping you and what are we going to form?"

The others were all looking at me expectantly.

"Well, erm, you're cheering me up with this sleepover, aren't you? And we're, erm, going to, erm, form, erm…"

"Cheerleaders!" Frankie exploded. "We're going to form a group of cheerleaders!"

"Great!" squealed Fliss.

"Fantastic!" screamed Rosie. "I've always wanted to be a cheerleader!"

I shot Frankie a nasty look and mouthed, "What have you done?"

She shrugged.

"Hey what about playing football?" I called, running to fetch a ball. "That's what we're here for. We won't bother about teams yet. For the moment it's every girl for herself!"

"Then can we be cheerleaders?" begged Fliss.

"Sure!" I agreed. "When we've finished our games."

We piled on to the makeshift pitch in the garden. The grass is a bit bare from where I run around on it so much, but we've got a proper set of goalposts and everything.

To start with, the football went really well. Fliss was hopeless, but then, what's new? But Rosie wasn't too bad at all. In fact, the more she played, the better she got. She even tried some pretty daring shots and that's really where the trouble started.

She did this one amazing shot which looped way up in the air and sort of did a banana bend at the last minute. *Ping!* It flew into the back of the net.

"That was amazing, Rosie!" I flung my arms round her. "To think I was worried about you playing in the team! If you play like that, we'll definitely walk off with the trophy!"

The others all stopped hugging and turned to stare at me. It was like a cross between a film and a bad dream – everything seemed to be happening in slow motion.

"What did you say?" asked Rosie at last.

I took a deep breath.

"I just said that when we enter that five-a-side competition, we'll have a good chance of winning it. Now that you're playing so well."

"Five-a-side team?" screamed Fliss. "That's why we're having this stupid football sleepover, isn't it? You were only thinking of yourself, as usual. You're a selfish cheat, Laura McKenzie! You dropped us for all that time just to play football, and now you're expecting us to help you out again. Well I've had enough!"

She stormed across the lawn and picked up her sleepover kit, which she'd dumped there earlier. Rosie ran after her and they both headed for the door.

This was supposed to be a fun sleepover, and it was turning into a disaster! Just as Frankie had predicted it would.

CHAPTER SIX

"Hey you guys, wait!" I flew across the lawn after them with Lyndz and Frankie in hot pursuit.

I reached the front door at the same time as Fliss and managed to lean my full weight against it so that it was impossible to open.

"What on earth's going on?" asked Mum, who had come out of the kitchen to investigate what all the noise was. "You're not going, are you Felicity? Rosie?"

"It's nothing Mum, just a misunderstanding," I reassured her. "We'll sort it out, don't worry."

"Well, if you're sure." She looked reluctant

to leave us. "Call me if you need me."

She went back into the kitchen, and as soon as we heard the door close, all hell let loose again.

"You should have told us about the five-a-side team," Rosie accused me. "*Especially* as we'd already told you that we weren't interested."

"But Kenny was only trying to show you how much fun it can be," Frankie tried to explain.

"Yeah, well, it's one thing having a kick-around in Kenny's garden, and quite another showing ourselves up in front of everyone else," Fliss muttered, but she didn't look quite so cross.

"I'm sorry, I was being selfish," I admitted. "I just wanted to play in that competition so badly. I guess I just assumed that as we're all friends, you wouldn't mind helping me out. I've always helped you out in the past, haven't I?"

The others looked at each other.

"We don't mind helping out, Kenny," Rosie

explained. "It's just that we're not very good at football."

"But you *are!*" I assured them. "And all Fliss needs is a bit of practice and a lot more confidence. Besides, she could work to our advantage. If we stick her in goal, the guys on the other teams will probably take one look at her, fall in love and forget that we're playing football!"

Fliss blushed and went all giggly which started the rest of us off. Fliss is such a total sucker for flattery. I swear to you, if ever you want a favour from her, just tell her she looks wonderful and she'll do whatever you ask! Easy!

"So Fliss, can we count you in?" asked Frankie.

Fliss looked round the others.

"I guess so," she said slowly. The rest of us cheered. "But if anyone laughs at me. I'm off. OK?"

"And is the sleepover back on?" I asked anxiously.

"*Yesss!*"

*   *   *

I thought that under the circumstances, it might be pushing it a bit if I made the others play football again, so you'll never guess what we did… We pretended to be cheerleaders! I know, I know – it was my idea of a nightmare, but it seems that Fliss had got it into her head that that's what she wanted to do. She sort of bribed me actually.

"If we can't be cheerleaders, I'm not playing in your stupid team," she pouted. You see, Fliss isn't as dumb as she looks. She's not above a bit of blackmail when it suits her.

I just felt such an idiot prancing about shouting:

"Cuddington five-a-side,
We're going to sweep the rest aside!
Give me a C, give me a U, give me a D…"

Well, you get the picture don't you? At least it kept Fliss happy. But I was relieved when Mum called us in for supper.

That was well cool too because we had lots of football-type food – hotdogs with onions (vegetarian for Frankie of course), those cheesy footballs and loads of crisps. Mum had iced some buns so that they looked like footballs, and she'd made some gingerbread footballers too. It was class!

After supper we went for a runabout in the garden again. Which was great until Molly the Monster turned up. She'd been out with her friend, and I'd expected her to stay out longer, but no such luck. Her friend probably got sick of her too. Anyway, she stormed out into the garden.

"I heard you lot screaming a mile away," she fumed. "It sounds like a kindergarten here."

"So?" I yelled back. "We're just having fun. But then you don't know what that is, do you?"

"Ha ha!" Molly stormed right up to me and started wagging her finger in front of my face. "You're pathetic, do you know that? You think you're this great big superstar. Well you live in a dream world. You'll never get anywhere playing football. You'll end up a nobody. I'm glad you can't play in that stupid competition. It would only make you even more big-headed."

71

I was just *so* mad. There was no way that I was going to let her get away with that. I lunged into her and wrestled her to the ground. You could tell that the others didn't know whether to join in or not, but I think they figured it was a family thing so they just hung back. I grabbed handfuls of Molly's hair and tugged as hard as I could until she was screaming, but as she had hold of my shoulders I couldn't do much else.

"What a display!" Dad stormed out and wrestled us apart. "I thought that you would have known better, especially when we have visitors. Whatever will they think?"

"She started it!" I muttered, but Dad was having none of it.

"I think you'd better go to your rooms. Sorry girls," he apologised to my friends, "but I think it's time for the sleeping part of this sleepover."

We headed for the door.

"Was that a demonstration of football hooliganism then?" Rosie whispered to me with a grin.

Molly walked past us, rubbing her head. "Loser!" she muttered.

"I don't think you'll be saying that when Kenny wins that football competition," Fliss called out ever so sweetly. "Because you see, we're going to be playing in a team with her after all!"

Now I'm not too big on hugging, as you know, but Fliss deserved a big bear hug for that.

"Gitoutofit!" She pretended to fight me off, but she had this huge grin on her face.

"Thanks Fliss. Thanks all of you!" I squealed when we got into my room. "I really do appreciate this."

"You'd better!" laughed Frankie.

"Yeah, we'll never let you forget it!" agreed Lyndz.

"But shouldn't we decide what we're going to wear?" asked Fliss. "I mean we can't turn up in just any old football kit, can we? We need something to get us noticed and *hey*…"

We all started bashing her with our pillows. I mean what is she like, bothering about our kits for goodness sake! She gave us the chance to have a really good squishy poo fight anyway. We hadn't done that for ages. We stuffed all our spare clothes in Lyndz's sleeping bag and tried to knock each other off the bed with it. Molly nearly had a fit when she came in to collect some of her stuff.

"Get off my bed... NOW!" she yelled at the top of her lungs.

"All right, keep your hair on!" I yelled back. "Your bed's not bouncy enough anyway, Miss Prissy-Pants!"

"Well just leave all my stuff alone, OK?" she spat menacingly, tidying up her side of the bedside table. We all sat quietly on my bed until she'd left, then exploded with laughter.

"Talk about control freak!" I shrieked. "It would serve her right if we spilt our midnight feast all over her precious things!"

The mention of food was all we needed to spur us on to get ready for bed. We wriggled out of our clothes inside our sleeping bags and did our pyjama shuffle into our jimjams. Then we raced to the bathroom to get there before stupid Molly the Monster. We had a great time preventing her from getting in. We usually wash and brush our teeth in about three minutes flat, but we managed to spin it out to about forty minutes just so she had to hang around. We would have been longer, but we heard her complaining to Dad downstairs. So we hurried back to my room as fast as we could and pretended to be tucked up in bed when he knocked on my door. I don't think he was fooled, but it was wicked just knowing how mad we'd made Molly!

Our midnight feast was class too. We were all really hyper, especially as everybody had brought those little chocolate footballs to eat. There was this huge mountain of them piled up on Frankie's sleeping bag. Every time someone took another bag of them out, the rest of us got hysterical. It was just *so* funny! When I'd calmed down a bit I tried to dribble one round the room, but I kept losing it and Fliss got really mad when I kept throwing one at her shouting:

"Here Fliss, save this!"

When we'd munched our way through most of them, Frankie suddenly moaned:

"I feel really sick now. I didn't think it was possible to eat too much chocolate."

"I know," groaned Fliss. "I'm going to have to lie down."

That kind of seemed like a good idea to all of us. I had planned to tell loads of football jokes, but I was feeling so icky I couldn't even think of one.

That must have been our quietest end to a sleepover *ever*. It was just a relief that no-one actually threw up. In the morning we were still feeling a bit green though, so we didn't even feel up to a practice game of football before the others left. I just hoped they realised that the five-a-side practice was on Wednesday, and that they'd have to hone their skills a bit before then.

It was certainly no good trying to make them practise at school the following week.

"Everybody will be watching us," moaned Fliss.

"But you'll have to play in front of other

people in the competition," I told her. "We can't have a private room, you know!"

"I know!" snapped Fliss. "I've been practising at home with Callum and Andy if you must know!"

I hoped Fliss was right because she certainly needed the practice. And of course Wednesday afternoon was the big moment of truth...

It had become a bit sort of obvious as Wednesday went on that Fliss was not looking forward to the practice at all.

"Don't worry, we'll all be there together," we'd tried to reassure her, but it didn't seem to work. Every time we looked at her she seemed to be getting greener and greener.

"Come on Fliss," I told her when the home-time bell finally went. "It's not as bad as all that. The boys will be fine, you'll see. And Mr Pownall's great."

"I... I don't care. I... I... I'm not going!" she stammered.

"Oh yes you are, my girl!" I shouted.

77

"Am *not*!"

"Come on Fliss," reasoned Rosie. "I'm worse than you and I'm going. If I hate it, well, I won't be going again." She flashed me a look. "But we won't know until we get there, will we?"

That sort of calmed Fliss down.

"OK, but if anyone laughs…."

"… you're out of there," the rest of us finished for her. "Yes, we know!"

When we got to the changing room I must admit that I was really excited. I couldn't wait to be playing football again, but I tried not to look too eager in front of the others.

"I hope Ryan Scott's not going to be a pain," Frankie whispered to me as we made our way into the gym. "Because Fliss means it, you know? One peep out of him and we won't see her for dust."

"He'll be fine!" I said confidently.

Why did I open my big mouth? As soon as we got into the gym, I kind of sensed that we'd made a big mistake. The boys were already warming up, but they stopped as soon as they saw us come in. One minute there was silence, the next the gym was echoing with the sound of loud guffawing.

"I know McKenzie can play a bit, but the rest of you girls…?" Ryan Scott was shrieking with laughter. "Do me a favour! You're having a laugh, aren't you?"

"Ignore them Fliss," I hissed. "Fliss?"

I looked round, but Fliss was nowhere to be seen. She'd done a disappearing act before we'd even started!

CHAPTER SEVEN

"Silence!" Mr Pownall yelled at the top of his voice. "How dare you be so rude!"

He went to stand in front of Ryan Scott, who had gone squashed-tomato red and was quivering in his boots.

"I take it you still want to play for the five-a-side team?" Mr Pownall asked him.

Scotty-chops nodded.

"Well then, I suggest that you apologise to these girls – now."

"Sorry," he muttered.

"We didn't quite hear that, did we girls?" Mr Pownall smiled over to us.

"No sir!"

"I'm very sorry that I was rude," Ryan said very slowly and clearly.

"Rude about what?" asked a voice.

"Fliss? Where've you been?" I shrieked.

"I had to go back to put my hair up again," she explained. "What have I missed?"

"Nothing Fliss, believe me!" I said, and breathed a big sigh of relief. Fliss hadn't walked out at all, and after Mr Pownall's speech the boys wouldn't dare laugh at us again. Re-*sult*!

Well, it wasn't quite as easy as that. As soon as we started our exercises it became pretty obvious that both Fliss and Rosie were strangers to football. Instead of dribbling with the ball, they spent most of their time chasing it round the gym because they had no control over it. Talk about embarrassing! To make matters worse, all the boys kept sort of spluttering whenever they saw them. Fliss and Rosie's confidence, fragile as it was, looked to be disappearing fast.

"Right girls!" smiled Mr Pownall eventually. "You're doing really well considering that you haven't played before. Let's leave those boys to their own devices for a while and get you sorted."

He was just great. He showed Fliss and Rosie how to control the ball and how to stop a shot. Then they practised passing to each other whilst Frankie, Lyndz and I did the same. Then the five of us got together and passed a football between ourselves. You couldn't believe that Fliss was the same person. I mean, she still did the odd dodgy pass and missed the ball a couple of times, but so what? You couldn't expect her to be as good as me after one lesson, now could you?! She was so much more confident anyway, and you know what? She actually looked as though she was *enjoying* herself.

The big challenge was the practice five-a-side match against the boys at the end of the session. It was the first time that Fliss had played in goal, and amazingly she wasn't bad at all. She's used to catching and throwing balls in netball you see, so that sort of helped her out. And besides, she didn't have any idea about the rules for normal football, so she picked up the ones for five-a-side in no time. I have to admit that I was well impressed. Rosie got stuck in too – talk about a mean tackler, she certainly didn't mess around!

We lost the match 3–2. I hate losing, especially to the boys, but Frankie did remind me that it was only a practice match.

"Well, what do you think?" I asked the others in the changing room afterwards.

"Great!"

"Cool!"

"When can we play again?" asked Fliss.

Well, I didn't need asking twice. Every lunchtime we went into the gym, and if Mr Pownall was around he gave us some more coaching, which was cool. So as the five-a-side practices came round each week, we were getting better and better and more and more confident.

Of course, the more we played, the more the boys were rude to us.

"You're not seriously going in for the competition, are you McKenzie?" Ryan Scott asked during our last practice. "You're going to embarrass yourselves. Why don't you stay at home and do some knitting or something?"

Of course his cronies cracked up about that.

"Don't worry about him," I told the others very loudly. "He can't even pass wind, never mind the ball!"

Everybody just creased up, even Danny McCloud. Scotty-chops turned bright pink and looked dead embarrassed. Fliss gave me a filthy look.

"You shouldn't embarrass him in front of his mates like that!" she scolded.

To sort of make up for it, she went all gooey in the goal whenever Ryan Scott took a shot. She let in every single one. I mean, she didn't even *try* to save them.

"Promise me you won't do that in the competition on Saturday," I warned her after the practice. "Because if you do, I swear that I'll chop off that precious blonde hair of yours with a knife and fork!"

"Give her a break." Frankie came to her rescue. "She's doing her best. The rest of us haven't been playing as long as you, remember."

"Yes, and the competition's on *Saturday*," squealed Lyndz. "Are you sure we're going to be ready for it?"

"'Course we are!" I reassured them. "We're just going to have to practise like crazy so we're ready to beat the pants off everybody!"

The others didn't look too sure.

"Never mind about practising!" said Fliss. "What are we going to wear?"

Typical! But she did have a point. None of us was too keen on Fliss's suggestion of baby pink T-shirts and bright pink shorts though.

"What about just a plain white T-shirt and navy shorts?" suggested Rosie. "We've all got those already."

"But how will anybody know which team we belong to?" asked Lyndz. "And what are we going to call ourselves anyway?"

Crikey, I didn't realise it was all going to be so complicated!

"What about Cuddington Girls?" suggested Frankie.

"Nah, too boring!"

"All right then – Sleepover Girls United?" she proposed. "Because we are, aren't we? United, I mean."

"Great idea, Frankie!" Rosie was really excited. "And we could embroider S.G.U. on our T-shirts to show which team we belong to!"

Hmm – sewing is not my strong point. I figured that writing it on with a felt pen would be good enough for me! Besides, I had far too much to do before the competition without thinking about soppy sewing. There was our training to organise for a start, and I had to sort out all the details for the competition. I was determined that absolutely *nothing* was going to go wrong.

I knew that there would be hundreds of people turning up on Saturday, so I figured that we needed to organise ourselves as much support as possible. Well, what a performance *that* turned out to be! Frankie's mum had her ante-natal classes on Saturday morning, and – wouldn't you know it? – Lyndz's mum was teaching them, so that would be two fewer people we could count on. I mean, everyone knows how to have babies, don't they? You'd think they could just skip the class for once. Fliss's mum had a hissy fit when she discovered that her precious baby was playing football and insisted on being there to make sure that she didn't come to any harm. And if you know Fliss's mum, you know that that's exactly the kind of support we didn't need. My mum said she'd be there and Dad would come along when he could, but there would be no Molly, thank goodness. Honestly, it was like trying to organise the FA Cup and Posh Spice's wedding all rolled into one.

The most important thing though was our training. And boy, did I put the others through their paces!

"I'm exhausted!" moaned Fliss on Friday night. "I'm not even going to have the energy to get up in the morning, never mind play football."

"Quit whingeing!" I told her. "We're going to win this competition and don't you forget it!"

Fliss looked terrified. In fact they all did.

"Look, if we play like we have been doing over the last week, we're capable of beating anyone. OK?"

"Yeah!"

We all stood in a circle and grabbed each other's right hands. We held them together then raised them into the air as fast as we could, shouting "Sleepover Superstars!" at the tops of our voices. It was class, but everybody else thought we were totally bonkers!

"See you tomorrow! Sleep well!" we all called out as we left each other. But of course none of us slept at all. I was just too pumped up. I wanted to get on with it and start playing football.

I'll never forget how I felt when I arrived at the Leisure Centre for the competition the next morning. My stomach was in knots and I felt kind of sick too but I was still totally hyper.

"I knew it was you jiggling about!" called

Frankie, running over to join me. "Dad said we should go inside to register – he's gone to hold us a place in the queue."

"I'll try to spot the others and send them in to you," Mum suggested, so Frankie and I headed inside.

But Frankie's dad wasn't in the queue. He was standing next to someone right at the front. It was Rosie! Apparently Adam had made her get there extra early because he was more excited than she was! We just joined her in time too, because she was about to give our name to the guy in charge.

"Sleepover Girls United!" we all said together.

"Oh, oh, I see," he spluttered, looking up at us. "Well, yes, we'll have to wait, there's time yet! You will be team number 9. Here are your numbers, pin them on to your shorts. Next!"

"What was he on about then?" I asked the others, handing round our numbers.

"I think he was getting a bit flustered because there are so many people," explained Rosie. "He's been like that with everyone."

"Talking of everyone, where are Lyndz and Fliss?" asked Frankie, anxiously scanning the crowds which were starting to build up.

"You know Lyndz, she's always late!" Rosie said.

"It's not Lyndz I'm worried about," I admitted. "It's Fliss. What if she's bottled out?"

"She wouldn't!" gasped Rosie. "Not after all our hard work."

"She'd better not," I warned.

"What's up with you lot?" Lyndz bounded up to us. "Who are we playing? Do we know yet?"

"Nobody, if Fliss doesn't hurry up," explained Frankie grimly.

"Maybe she's lost in all these crowds," suggested Lyndz.

There were certainly hundreds of people, and it was hard to tell who were players and who were supporters.

Suddenly a big siren sounded.

"Can I have your attention please," announced a voice over the loudspeaker.

"Would all competitors please make their way to the playing arena, and could all spectators make sure that they are standing well behind the barriers."

I looked around and saw Mum, Frankie's dad, Rosie's mum, Adam and Lyndz's dad with Ben and Spike. They were all waving and giving us the thumbs-up.

"Where is Fliss?" I was getting really agitated now.

"She'll be here," Frankie tried to reassure me.

When it was just the teams and not the spectators, there didn't seem to be quite so many people. The flustered guy was explaining how the competition would work. Four matches would be played at a time, and their results would be noted. It was a straightforward knockout format, with the winners of each match going on to the next round. There were sixteen teams, so the whole thing was going to take some time.

"If Fliss doesn't turn up soon, we'll be disqualified," I hissed.

The man started telling everyone who they would be playing.

"If we're not one of the first teams to play we'll have a bit more time," Lyndz whispered. "Keep your fingers crossed."

I could see Ryan Scott and the others standing around. They were team number 4. The guy had just two team numbers left to call out for the first four matches.

"Pick number 4, pick number 4," I chanted.

"Number 7 – that's Ashley Park Boys."

Phew!

"And number… 9. Ah, Sleepover Girls United. Where are they please?"

My heart sank.

CHAPTER EIGHT

"Sleepover Girls United? That's me! I mean that's us. Sorry I'm late!" Fliss came flying through the crowds. "It was my hair, and my make-up, and, oh never mind – I'm here now. Who are we playing?"

The guy in charge was open-mouthed. So were the rest of us. Not only was Fliss gabbling ten to the dozen, she was also done up like a dog's dinner. She'd sewn the initials S.G.U. on her T-shirt in *sequins*, for goodness sake.

"Erm, I think we're playing Ashley Park Boys. Is that right?" I turned to the guy.

"Well, you see, I'm afraid, well, the thing is,"

he spluttered. "Well, I'm afraid you won't be playing anybody."

"*What?*" we all yelled together.

"Look, Fliss is only a *bit* late," reasoned Frankie. "Surely that doesn't matter?"

"No, the problem is that there are no more girls' teams registered," the guy explained. "And I'm afraid the rules are that girls can only play against other girls. I'm really sorry."

I couldn't *believe* it! All that training for nothing!

"You'd have thought that Mr Pownall would have told us that," Lyndz growled in frustration.

"I thought that other girls' teams would be playing in the competition." Mr Pownall suddenly appeared behind us. "In fact, my friend from Hollymount School was supposed to be bringing a team of girls along, I don't know what's happened to him. I was sure that you'd have at least one game. Besides, you were so enthusiastic about the whole thing, I didn't want to put you off."

I felt *totally* gutted. The others looked pretty

devastated too. Apart from Fliss. A stupid smile of relief kept playing on her lips, and she had to try really hard to pretend that she was as miserable as the rest of us.

"Come on love, cheer up. I'm sure there'll be another competition soon," Mum came over to console me.

"No there won't," I grumbled. "Nobody wants girls to play football. It's not *fair*!"

"You sound just like Fliss!" Frankie whispered, trying to cheer me up.

"That's not funny," I muttered.

"Come on Kenny, we might as well support the guys now we're here," suggested Rosie.

"Yes!" Fliss squealed. "We could be their cheerleaders! Come on!"

Before I knew where I was, the others had dragged me right next to the pitch where Ryan and Danny and the others were playing their first match.

"Cuddington Boys can really play,

They're going to blow the rest away!" Fliss began.

"Give me a C!"

"C!" shouted the others.

"Give me a U!"

Talk about embarrassing! I thought the boys were going to die when they heard them at first. It certainly rocked their concentration a bit, especially when Fliss started making up all these crazy dance moves for the others to follow. I thought Mr Pownall might be a bit annoyed too, but he just smiled and pretended he was conducting them.

"Come on Kenny, don't be a spoilsport!" Frankie danced up to me. "You should join in too!"

But to tell you the truth I just didn't feel like it. I tried to concentrate on the football. The boys were 1–0 up, but Ryan Scott was passing the ball like a donkey and giving it to the opposition far too much.

"Pass it out to Danny on the wing!" I kept yelling.

And of course when he followed my advice it worked a treat. They won their match 3–1.

"Thanks Kenny, your advice seemed to do the trick." Mr Pownall came up to me when their match was over. "Maybe you'd like to be my co-manager for the rest of the competition?"

I thought he was being sarcastic at first, but he was dead serious.

"I guess I could," I told him. "It'll get me out of being a cheerleader, anyway!"

As soon as we found out who our boys would be facing in the next round, Mr Pownall and I worked out our tactics. Ryan Scott wasn't too happy about me being involved, but when he saw that I knew what I was talking about he accepted it. Especially when they made it through to the final. The cheerleading went down a storm too. The guys in the team acted like they were big Premier League superstars and lapped up all the attention. And the atmosphere for the final was just *electric* as the crowd joined in with the chants too!

"The team you're up against has got a big gorilla at the back," I warned the boys in the team talk before they went on the pitch. "You'll have to watch him and try to dummy-pass around him because he'll flatten you if you get too close."

"Right boss!" they all nodded, like I was some hot-shot manager or something. It was cool. I mean I'd rather have been playing, but this was the next best thing.

By half-time the score was 1–1 and the boys looked to be on top of things. They scored again just after half-time, but the other team equalised straight away.

"Watch the gorilla!" I kept yelling. "Watch the gorilla!"

With about thirty seconds to go, it looked as though there was going to be extra time, but the gorilla bundled into Ryan Scott. Ryan took the free kick and their goalkeeper came out of his area to collect the ball.

"Penalty!"

We were all going wild.

"Let Danny take it!" I yelled.

Ryan stepped up with the ball.

"Let Danny take it!" I yelled again.

Ryan took the kick, missed, the goalkeeper collected the ball, rolled it out to the gorilla who lumbered up the pitch and...

"Oh no, he's scored!"

Screee! The whistle went for full time. The guys had lost and I felt gutted for the second time that day. I couldn't believe it.

"I told Scotty to let Danny take the penalty," I moaned to the others afterwards. "It's all his fault."

"Oh come on now, that's not fair," said Frankie.

"I bet Ryan's feeling awful now," Lyndz agreed. "I feel really sorry for him."

The only person I was feeling sorry for was myself. I'd been cheated out of playing in the competition, and I felt as though I'd been cheated out of being the winning manager too.

Fortunately, I'd got over it a bit by Monday morning when we got to school. I even managed to mumble "Bad luck, you played really well" to the guys in the team. But I just couldn't face playing football. In fact I couldn't face playing football for the rest of the week, and there was no way on earth that I was going to turn up to the five-a-side practice on Wednesday. What would be the point?

"I think you might be taking this too seriously," Frankie suggested. "Why can't you still play football for fun, like you used to?"

"It's not the same," I tried to explain. "I just feel cheated that we never got the chance to prove how good we are."

"How good *you* are, you mean!" laughed Lyndz. "I don't think the rest of us would have been much good in a competition."

"We'll never know, will we?" I told her sadly. "Anyway, are you going to the practice?"

"We can't without you, can we?" Rosie pointed out. "We wouldn't have a team."

I knew that they were trying to make me feel guilty, but my mind was made up – I wasn't going. Fliss looked quite relieved anyway.

Well, on the Thursday, I was just minding my own business in the playground before school when a football rolled on to my foot. I looked around, but I couldn't see where it might have come from. The others hadn't arrived yet so it couldn't be them. I could see Ryan and Danny kicking a ball about over on the field, but they were too far away.

"Come on then Kenny, pass it back!" It was Mr Pownall. "It's not like you not to kick the ball back."

"I'm sorry sir, I couldn't work out where it had come from," I explained.

Mr Pownall walked over to me.

"You weren't at five-a-side practice yesterday," he said. "Don't tell me you've given up on it?"

"There didn't seem much point in coming, after the fiasco at the competition," I sighed. "If we're never going to get a game, what's the point in playing?"

"And is that what your friends think?" he asked.

"Dunno," I shrugged. "I think they were only entering the competition for my benefit, because they knew how much I wanted to play."

"Very noble!" laughed Mr Pownall. "But they enjoyed playing too, didn't they? They were getting quite good."

"Yes, they were," I admitted.

"So they'd be quite happy to play in a competition if I organised one with a girls' team then?" he asked.

"Yes, but you're never going to find one, are you?"

"Well Miss McKenzie, that's where you're wrong!" Mr Pownall beamed. "You know I told you that my friend should have been taking a team from Hollymount School to the competition? Well, their minibus broke down on the way there, and one of the girls was sick so they never made it. Now his girls are hungry for a competition too. So we've arranged one for you all here – next Wednesday. What do you say? Are you up for it?"

I couldn't say anything. For once I was speechless. All I could do was grin like an idiot. In fact I was still opening and closing my mouth like a goldfish when the others appeared.

"What's up with you?" asked Frankie, prodding me in the ribs.

"Are you ill?" Rosie felt my head.

"Stop doing that, Kenny!" commanded Fliss. "You're freaking me out!"

It was just hysterical, them fussing over me like that. I cracked up laughing.

"I think she's really lost it this time," Lyndz whispered behind her hand.

That made me laugh even more. I started leaping around and punching the air.

"It's OK, it's OK!" I yelled. "We've got ourselves a competition!"

The others all looked at each other then back at me.

"Game on!"

CHAPTER NINE

Well, you can imagine how totally hyper we were about the competition. This was going to be our chance to prove ourselves. But after we'd played football together that lunchtime, I started to have my doubts about the whole thing. I mean, it had been less than a week since we'd last played together, but the others seemed to have forgotten absolutely everything that Mr Pownall had taught them. And what made it worse was that they just laughed about it.

"Whoops, butterfingers!" Fliss giggled as she scooped the ball out of the net for about the tenth time.

"Concentrate for goodness sake!" I yelled. "This competition is serious, you know."

"Lighten up, Kenny!" Frankie rugby-tackled me to the ground. The others all piled on top of us and started tickling me.

"Get off!" I gasped, struggling to get up. "It's not funny, we've got to practise for the match."

"You're a right misery guts, do you know that?" Rosie grumbled, scrambling up from the ground.

"Look, I'm sorry," I said. "But I thought you wanted to win this match as much as I do. This might be our only chance to play, and wouldn't it be great to go out in a blaze of glory?"

"Well, yes," admitted Lyndz, "but I don't suppose there'll be anyone watching us anyway. It's not a big competition like last Saturday, is it?"

"But we don't need supporters to play well, do we?" I fired back. "You're just being defeatist. Come on guys, do it for me?"

The others all looked at each other.

"OK, but we're only doing it this once,"

Frankie spoke for all of them.

"And if anyone laughs at me..." piped up Fliss.

"... you're out of there," the rest of us said together. "Yes, we know!"

The problem was that to practise properly we really needed some opposition. We tried practising by ourselves over the weekend, but it got pretty hopeless. I mean, when you're trying to be the striker *and* the goalkeeper you can get a bit of an identity crisis!

"This is never going to work!" wailed Fliss. "We're going to be a laughing stock. We'll have to call the whole thing off!"

"No way!" I told her. "We'll just have to sort something out!"

And that's where the boys came in. (I always knew that they must be useful for something!) It nearly made me choke to ask them a favour on Monday morning, but it had to be done.

"But boys aren't supposed to play against girls," sneered Ryan Scott when I finally asked him to play against us. "You might get too upset when you never get the ball."

"Yeah, right!" I snorted. "I reckon you're scared that we're going to beat the pants off you. Not up to the challenge then, Scotty Boy?"

"OK, you're on!" he said indignantly, "but you'd better not start snivelling when we keep beating you!"

As if!

I knew that Fliss would have a fit when I told her what I'd arranged, so I didn't tell her until the last minute. Bad move! She nearly wet herself when she saw Ryan Scott all puffed up waiting for the contest.

"I… I can't play against them!" she wailed.

"'Course you can," I told her firmly. "You've done it before. Just forget who they are. Pretend they're girls or something."

Easier said than done. Fliss just froze every time she saw Ryan Scott with the ball. 1–0, the ball flew into the goal over her head. 2–0, the ball whizzed in past her left hand. 3–0, the ball whooshed in to her right. 4–0, the ball whipped in through her legs.

"Come on Fliss, get a grip!" I yelled. I turned

to Frankie. "This is hopeless!"

"Hang on a minute, I've got an idea," she said.

She quietly went over to have a word with Ryan Scott, and when she'd whispered something else to Fliss she came back.

"Right, I reckon the rest of us should have a bit of shooting practice, what do you say?" she said, and grabbing another football, she went towards the other goal.

"What's going on?" I asked her when Danny McCloud and the others were shooting at goal.

"Oh, I just told Scotty what a great striker he is."

I stared at her in disbelief.

"And said that because he's such a superstar," she continued, "he's the only person we can rely on to give Fliss the practice she needs."

"*What?*" I shrieked. "You traitor! What about Girl Power? I'm better than Ryan Scott any day of the week. And you know it!"

"I know," agreed Frankie. "But would Fliss have listened to you like that?" She gestured to where Fliss was engrossed in what Ryan Scott was telling her.

"I guess not," I agreed. "But he'll be so big-headed now, he'll be unbearable. I hope it's worth it!"

Well, I was definitely right about him getting big-headed. He never stopped rubbing it in that we needed his help to sort out our playing. I was well annoyed about that.

"I'm going to kill you for this!" I warned Frankie. "He's more unbearable than ever."

"I know!" she agreed. "I made a BIG mistake with that. You'd better shoot me now!"

Of course Fliss was absolutely delirious about Ryan Scott's attention, which just made us madder still.

"I bet she hasn't learnt *anything* from him," Rosie said before our match against the boys the next lunchtime. "She's probably just been batting her eyelashes at him and telling him how wonderful he is!"

Well, that's where we were all wrong. Fliss played an absolute blinder in goal. Nothing got past her. And we actually won the game 1–0!

"Hey Fliss, you were brilliant!" we all congratulated her afterwards.

"She had a good coach, didn't she?" smirked Ryan Scott from behind us. "Good job you've got a man like me to sort you out, isn't it?"

"*Man?!*" we snorted. "In your dreams, mate!"

"Don't get too cocky," he sneered. "We only let you win because Pownall said we had to boost your confidence."

"Yeah right!" I laughed.

"You don't think he was serious, do you?" asked Rosie anxiously afterwards.

"No way! We won that fair and square," I reassured her. I was sure that they would never let us win a game like that. Although it did play on my mind just a teensy bit on Wednesday as we got ready for the competition…

Boy, was it tough getting through *that* day. We were all so nervous we could barely talk to each other, never mind do things like work and eat. Fliss lost it completely – surprise, surprise!

"I can't do this!" she kept whimpering. "I'm sorry, I just can't."

"Yes you can!" I told her firmly. "We all promised that we'd do it this once. Besides, we've already beaten the boys' team. How frightening can a girls' team be?"

"But the boys let us win, didn't they?" she twittered.

I was going to make mincemeat of stupid Ryan Scott when I got hold of him.

"At least there'll be nobody there to watch us make fools of ourselves," muttered Lyndz.

She certainly seemed right there. Mrs Poole did mention the match in assembly and wished us luck, but nobody else seemed very interested. The M&Ms of course sneered at us, but what's new? They're our deadly rivals in everything, so you wouldn't exactly expect them to be cheering us on. But I thought that Danny McCloud and Ryan Scott might have mentioned it. After all, we had supported them in their competition. But that's boys for you, I guess.

Anyway, when the bell went at home time,

we all made our way into the changing rooms. By that time I was feeling more than a little sick. Part of me was desperate to get on with the match, and part of me wished that we'd never got involved in the five-a-side thing to start with.

"Just think, in less than twenty minutes it will all be over!" said Frankie grimly, pulling her T-shirt over her head. She'd embroidered S.G.U. on hers in big loopy silver letters. I'd used a black felt tip on mine.

"Couldn't you do better than that?" asked Fliss, looking at it. The sequins on hers were still sparkling. But to be honest with you, our T-shirts were really the last of our worries.

There was a knock at the door. Mr Pownall popped his head round it.

"Are you ready, girls? The other team's waiting for you."

We must all have looked petrified, because he laughed.

"There's nothing to worry about – treat it as just another game. Keep your concentration, use all the pitch and keep your defence tight at the back. I'll be there to shout instructions, so just enjoy yourselves!"

That made us feel a bit better.

"OK sir, we'll be out in a minute," I told him.

When he'd gone, we got into a group huddle.

"We're all in this together so let's go out and win this baby!"

We broke free and put our right hands into the centre.

"Sleepover Superstars!" we yelled, raising our hands into the air.

With that, we were really pumped up and ready for anything. We burst through the changing room doors into the gym and...

"I don't believe it!" gasped Frankie.

The gym was absolutely *packed* with people. There were children from every other year in the school, loads of teachers – even Mrs Poole was there. But there were just as many people who we didn't recognise. They must have come with the other team.

"Blimey!" shrieked Rosie. "Look at them!"

On the pitch were some of the meanest-looking girls we'd ever seen. And *huge*! They looked like Teletubbies in football shorts!

"We are going to get slaughtered!" wailed Fliss. Lyndz just started to hiccup, which is Lyndz's response to any crisis. Frankie tried to deal with her whilst I tried hard to think how we should approach the game. And that's when the cheerleading started. At first all we could hear was Mr Pownall's voice warbling:

"Sleepover Superstars are the best,

They're going to score more than the rest!"

Then you could just hear a few more voices joining in.

"Give me an S…"

It was Ryan Scott and the others, can you believe that? They looked *dead* embarrassed too. I nearly cracked up. Mr Pownall must have made them do it – it was wicked!

I turned to the others.

"Right, we're going to win this, OK?" I told them firmly. "I know that they look a lot bigger than us, but that probably means that they're a lot slower. Don't let them intimidate you.

And Fliss, you've got to remember whatever it was that Scotty taught you, OK?"

She nodded, the others nodded, Lyndz hiccuped.

"Right, deep breaths and – we're on!"

We ran on to the pitch looking as though we were scared of nothing and nobody. It was a major act, but it boosted our confidence. The supporters went wild. It was totally awesome. I couldn't believe that they were cheering for us, but I couldn't let myself think about that too much. We had a football match to win!

It didn't start too well. In fact it was a disaster. We were 2–0 down in less than a minute. I was pushed out of the way by the huge girl I was marking and Fliss's brain had gone walkabout, so they scored from the kick-off. Then the exact same thing happened from the re-start. After their second goal, I heard one of their players say to her mate:

"This is a piece of cake!"

And I saw red. No way, NO WAY was I going to let them think that we were a walkover.

"Come on Sleepovers!" I clapped my hands

to gee the others up. "We can get back into this!"

The referee, who was a friend of Mr Pownall's, blew his whistle to re-start, and I passed back to Lyndz. She dummied past one of their players, Frankie shook off her marker, got the ball, passed to me and— *Wham!* 2–1.

I think they realised then that they had a game on their hands, and really tightened things up. Have you ever tried getting away from a bad-tempered hippopotamus in a hurry? I thought not. Well that's how it felt trying to shake off my marker. Every time I got the ball and tried to run down the pitch with it, I was bundled over. A couple of times the referee awarded us a foul against her, but their goalkeeper was like an octopus and seemed to be able to save anything that came at her. Fortunately for us, Fliss was holding her own in our goal.

When half-time came round, the score was still 2–1.

"It's hopeless!" mumbled Rosie. "We just can't get the ball."

"I, hic, know!" agreed Lyndz. "They're such, hic, bruisers, they just keep bundling us out of the, hic, way!"

"Just stick with it!" I urged them. "We'll get the chance to score, you'll see!"

"But we've only got another six minutes," Frankie muttered. "We're going to need longer than that."

"Don't give up!" I told them firmly. "We need you to be strong, Fliss. If you can keep them out, then we've got a chance to win this match!"

The whistle blew for the start of the second half, and the opposition came out with all guns blazing. We hardly got a look in. Ryan Scott was shouting instructions, but it was kind of hard to hear him over the din of all the supporters. When Lyndz finally got the ball he yelled:

"Pass it to Kenny!"

I heard him and managed to dodge past my marker. I got the ball and shot it as hard as I could. *Thud!* It shot into the back of the net just under the goalkeeper's diving body.

The crowd went wild. We were on level terms again! Two–all, two–all!

"We can win this!" I urged the others. "Come on, we can win this!"

But before we could compose ourselves, the other team had kicked off and the ball was heading towards our goal. Lyndz backtracked, their forward powered on… and only had Fliss to beat.

"It's yours, Fliss!" I screamed. "Grab it!"

We could only watch in horror as Fliss and their forward collided with a sickening thud.

CHAPTER TEN

My heart was in my mouth. I know it sounds awful, but I couldn't really think about Fliss. All I knew was that she'd just given away a penalty – we were done for. But then I saw the awful truth. The ball was already in the back of our net! It must have squirmed under her body when she collided with their player. The other team was going wild.

Screee! The referee blew his whistle and shook his head. "No goal, it was taken inside the area!" he told us, pointing for a free kick.

I looked to Fliss to take it, but she was still on the ground.

"Get up, Fliss, come on!" I urged. Trust her to be so dramatic.

"I can't," she squealed. "I think I've sprained my ankle."

I bent down to examine it while the others crowded round. Mr Pownall rushed on to the pitch and felt Fliss's ankle too.

"Well you haven't broken it, but it seems like a nasty sprain to me," he said. That had been my diagnosis too.

"It looks like that's it then," he said, shaking his head. "With no substitutes, we'd better call a halt to the match."

"NO!" we gasped.

"How many minutes are there left?" asked Frankie.

The referee looked at his watch. "Just over two," he replied.

"Can one of us go in goal?" asked Rosie.

"Well, yes," Mr Pownall replied, "but that will mean you're short in the outfield. Why don't we just ask for a rematch when Fliss has recovered? I'm sure Hollymount won't mind."

"I can hold out for two minutes," Fliss said

bravely, struggling to her feet. "I think we can win this match, and I'm not giving up now!"

We all hugged her, despite her wincing and squealing, "Mind my foot!"

I took charge of the tactics.

"Tighten up the defence at the back!" I told Rosie and Lyndz. "We'll have to protect Fliss as much as possible."

From the re-start it was clear that Hollymount Girls were going for the kill. It was like being charged down by a herd of hungry rhinoceros. Poor Fliss, she had this look of total panic in her eyes. After one close shave, when Lyndz had only just managed to prevent their player from shooting on target, Fliss whispered:

"Please score Kenny, because there's no way I can get through extra time!"

Talk about pressure! Time was fast running out and we needed a goal. I must have let my concentration slip for a second as I was planning how to score one, because one minute I had the ball, the next I'd given it away. I could see the others at sixes and sevens all over the pitch, and Hollymount's striker was in an acre of space. She was bound to score. THWACK! The ball thundered towards Fliss. There was no way she could save it!

"Dive, Fliss!" I heard Ryan yelling. "To your left!"

Fliss leapt the full width of the goal. She looked to have got down too late but the ball hit her leg and flew back out of the goalmouth. *Coo-ell!!*

"Way to go, Fliss!" I yelled. But I could see that she was clutching her ankle in agony.

When the ball had bounced out, Rosie had got it and was streaking down the pitch with it. I was caught between wanting to help Fliss and scoring a goal. Frankie was out on the wing, and Rosie found her with a perfect pass. But I could see two Hollymount girls rushing to tackle her.

"Over here, Frankie!" I yelled, and sprinted up the pitch, with Fliss screaming "Go Kenny!" behind me.

Frankie tried to cross the ball but it ricocheted off one of Hollymount's players –

right into the path of Rosie. She had a perfect sight of goal and nobody marking her.

"*Shoot!*" yelled Ryan Scott and Danny McCloud.

"*Shoot!*" yelled Frankie, Lyndz and Fliss.

I could hardly bear to look. Rosie had never been good at shooting practice and she looked to be panicking too much. It was all happening too fast, but at the same time it all seemed to be in slow motion. I saw her take her foot back, I saw the ball bobbling about and…

"GOOOAAALLL!"

She'd scored! I rushed over to her and flung my arms round her.

"I don't believe I did that!" she was gasping. She almost looked as though she was going to cry.

"We've got to keep it together until the whistle goes!" I told the others when we'd calmed down a bit.

And let me tell you, that was the longest minute of my life. I felt as though I could have walked into Leicester and back before the referee finally blew for time.

As you can imagine, as soon as we heard it we just went crazy. You'd have thought we'd won the World Cup or something! The crowd rushed on to the pitch and all these people engulfed us. It was totally awesome. Even Fliss forgot about her ankle so that she could join in with the celebrations too.

We didn't forget to commiserate with the other team though. We finally caught up with them in the changing room afterwards and shook their hands and told them how well they'd played. They all looked pretty down, so we tried not to get too hyper about winning the match.

"Shouldn't we exchange shirts or something?" I asked their captain.

She looked at my shirt. "Erm, I don't think so," she said, screwing up her nose.

I looked down, and my shirt was one massive swirl of black and grey where the felt tip S.G.U. had all run together. I *was* kind of hot and a bit sticky.

"If you think that's bad, you should see your face!" Frankie laughed.

I ran to the mirror. I looked like a chimney sweep! I must have got the ink from my shirt all over my hands and then smeared it all over my face.

"You look gross!" laughed Fliss.

"Yeah! That's why we got the ball so much at the end!" shrieked Rosie. "They probably thought you were the swamp monster or something!"

"I'm, hic, glad we didn't have to, hic, play extra time," Lyndz hiccuped. "I don't think I could have held out."

"*You* couldn't have held out!" Fliss snorted. "Just think about how I felt with my sprained ankle! And I pulled off a blinding save too. Did you see? It hurt like anything, but I did it!"

Frankie and I exchanged glances – we were never going to hear the end of Fliss's heroics. It didn't help matters that when we had got changed and went back into the gym, most of the crowd were still there. They started cheering again as soon as they saw us.

"Let's hear it for Sleepover Girls United!" shouted Mr Pownall. "Hip hip…"

"Hooray!" everybody shouted.

"Hip hip…"

"Hooray!" Even Ryan Scott was joining in, kind of reluctantly.

"Hip hip…"

"Hooray!" Mrs Poole was cheering, and so was my mum, Lyndz's mum, Frankie's mum and Fliss's mum. Rosie's mum appeared with Adam right at the last minute.

"I didn't know you were all coming!" I stared at them open-mouthed.

"We didn't tell you just in case we couldn't make it!" Mum laughed. "Congratulations!"

"I'm so proud of you all!" Frankie's mum looked as though she was about to cry and that wasn't like her. It must have been because of the baby and everything. Pregnancy makes your hormones go funny, you know.

"Wait until we tell your brothers!" Lyndz's mum was rubbing Lyndz's hand to get rid of the hiccups.

"Oh my poor brave baby!" squeaked Fliss's mum, examining Fliss's ankle. "I'm going to get you home and look at this properly. I hope you haven't damaged anything!" And with that Fliss was whisked away.

"It's a wonder she didn't run on to the pitch when Fliss fell down!" I mumbled.

"She tried to," Mum said. "We had to stop her, didn't we?"

Frankie and Rosie's mums looked at each other and they all cracked up laughing. Parents, eh? You can't take them anywhere!

After the match it was all a bit of an anticlimax really. We'd been building up to the competition for so long, and suddenly it was all over and we all felt a bit flat. Mrs Poole did call us out in assembly and everybody gave us a clap, but that was it. I wonder if footballers feel like this when they've won the FA Cup?

Look, the others are coming. We can give you an action replay of the whole match if you want. Fliss's ankle has finally recovered now, so she'll be able to show you how she dived to save that shot (she's been boring us about that ever since!). And you'd better not get Rosie started about how she scored the winning goal, you'll be here all night! Lyndz is dying for us to play in another match so that her brothers can come and watch. She says that they still don't believe that she can really play football. And Frankie keeps reminding me that I owe her a big favour for getting the others involved in the five-a-side competition to start with. I mean, come on, we won didn't we? Isn't that favour enough? She says that it's not exactly what she had in mind!

Now you just stay there and we'll demonstrate our footballing skills for you. And don't forget that:

WE ARE THE CHAMPIONS!